For Kurt Vandenberg, the best scientific adviser in the universe; and for Jordan Hamessley, the agent who always shoots for the stars—CH & EV

To Christy, for helping me navigate this new world and always being a great support!!!!!—GR

PENGUIN WORKSHOP
An Imprint of Penguin Random House LLC, New York

Text copyright © 2021 by Catherine Hapka and Ellen Vandenberg. Illustrations copyright © 2021 by Penguin Random House LLC. All rights reserved. Published by Penguin Workshop, an imprint of Penguin Random House LLC, New York. PENGUIN and PENGUIN WORKSHOP are trademarks of Penguin Books Ltd, and the W colophon is a registered trademark of Penguin Random House LLC. Manufactured in China.

Visit us online at www.penguinrandomhouse.com.

Library of Congress Cataloging-in-Publication Data is available.

ISBN 9780593095744 (paperback)   10 9 8 7 6 5 4 3 2 1
ISBN 9780593095751 (library binding)   10 9 8 7 6 5 4 3 2 1

Astronaut Girl

Girl STAR POWER

by Cathy Hapka and
Ellen Vandenberg
illustrated by Gillian Reid

Penguin Workshop

Chapter 1

RAINY DAY

"Look, Val." Wallace held up his notebook. "What do you think?"

I was watching the rain come down in Wallace's front yard. I looked at his notebook. There was a weird drawing in it.

"What is that thing?" I asked.

"It's a heat blaster," Wallace said. He pointed to the homemade action figure sitting on the porch swing. "Zixtar could use this to fight the ice aliens."

1

"It looks like a flying hot dog," I said. "What's the power source? Ketchup?"

My stomach grumbled. Hot dogs and ketchup made me think about the barbecue happening soon. All of Wallace's relatives were coming, and the whole neighborhood was invited, too. I couldn't wait. I just hoped it stopped raining by then.

"Whatever," Wallace muttered. "I'm just saying we need to figure something out, or the earth will be a giant snowball forever."

I shrugged. "We can figure it out after the barbecue."

He looked unhappy. I wasn't surprised. Wallace was obsessed with the TV show *Comet Jumpers*. He was even entering a contest to write an episode for the show!

Zixtar was a new character he'd created. That's what Wallace told me when he moved here last week. He doesn't know much about science or outer space, but lucky for him, I do! That's why everyone calls me Astronaut Girl. And it's why I offered to be his partner to write the script.

"Hey, Walla Walla!" someone shouted.

A car had just stopped in front of the house. "Who's that?" I asked. I couldn't wait to meet all of Wallace's relatives.

"It's Aunt Celia, Uncle Walt, and my cousins Kayla and Dwayne." Wallace still sounded grumpy. I wondered if he was worried about the barbecue being rained out. I wasn't worried, though. His gramps already said he would move the grill onto the back porch if he had to.

The adults waved and went inside. Dwayne and Kayla stayed on the porch. They were a few years older than us.

"Hi, I'm Val," I said. "I live next door. I'm Wallace's writing partner."

Dwayne grinned. "Writing partner, huh?" he said, and elbowed Wallace. "Is she going to help you not embarrass yourself at the family storytelling contest today?"

Dwayne and Kayla laughed. Wallace didn't.

"Storytelling contest?" I said. "What's that?"

They told me they had a family tradition. When everyone got together, they ended the gathering by holding a contest. Anyone who wanted to could tell a story, and everyone voted on the best one.

"I won at Easter dinner," Dwayne said. He held up the big fancy medal that hung from his neck. "I told the story about how I found a lost puppy when I was mountain biking. Everyone loved it."

Kayla nodded. "And at Thanksgiving, Aunt Kim won with this wild tall tale about a haunted henhouse. We couldn't stop laughing!"

I laughed, too. "That sounds fun!"

Wallace wasn't laughing. "Everyone else will be here soon," he said. "I should go see if Gramps needs help with the grill." He stomped off into the house.

"Oops, that reminds me," I told Dwayne and Kayla. "I promised Mom and Daddy I'd help with the potato salad. See you soon!"

I ran home through the rain. Mom and

Daddy were in the kitchen. Mom was scrubbing the potatoes, and Daddy was mixing herbs into the mayonnaise. The Baby was helping by tossing Cheerios at Astro Cat.

"Hi, Val," Daddy said. "You're just in time to peel the eggs."

I washed my hands and got to work. "I hope the sun comes out soon," I said. "Wallace seems kind of grumpy about the rain."

Mom looked surprised. "Really?" she said. "Wallace doesn't seem like the grumpy type."

The Baby giggled and tossed a handful of Cheerios at Daddy. A few landed in the mayonnaise bowl.

"That's not part of the recipe!" Daddy exclaimed with a laugh.

Suddenly the door flew open. Wallace rushed in.

"I just had a great idea for the script!" he cried. "We need to discuss it right now!"

Chapter 2

LAB WORK

"Now?" I said. "But the barbecue is starting soon."

I looked out the window. More cars were parked in front of Wallace's house. People were hurrying inside.

Daddy looked outside, too. "The sun's coming out just in time!"

"The sun is what we need to talk about, Val!" Wallace exclaimed. "I just remembered an idea that my friend Carlos

from back home had. He said Zixtar could hide from the ice aliens on the sun. While he's there, he can use the heat to power his blaster ray!"

I burst out laughing. Astro Cat stared at me in surprise.

"You have to be kidding," I told Wallace.

"Nobody can survive on the sun!"

"Well, we have to think of something!" Wallace said. "The deadline for the contest is only a couple of weeks away!"

Daddy winked at me. "We can finish up the potato salad without you. You and Wallace might need to review some data down in your lab."

Daddy always talks like that. He's an astrophysicist. That's a scientist who studies outer space, like I do.

"I guess you're right. Come on, Wallace," I said.

"Hang on," Mom said. She picked up the Baby and handed him to me. "Take him with you, or there will be more Cheerios than potatoes in the salad."

I took the Baby and led Wallace to the basement. Astro Cat tagged along.

My lab has everything a scientist like me needs. There's a table where I draw blueprints and a whiteboard for making calculations. I have tools to build stuff and lots of cabinets and drawers. Everything is labeled with my state-of-the-art label maker. Some of my projects are on display, like my mobile of the solar system that won a prize in the science fair.

The Baby uses part of my lab as a playroom. I put him in his playpen with the stuffed rocket ship I gave him.

Wallace sat down on a stool. "So what about Carlos's idea? I think it's great."

"*Great?*" I said. "No way. It's a good thing I'm your writing partner now instead of Carlos."

Wallace scowled. "Don't insult my friend."

"I'm not insulting anyone," I said. "Facts

are facts. And a star like the sun is the last place someone would hide out. For one thing, the surface temperature is almost ten thousand degrees Fahrenheit, and—"

"Wait," Wallace interrupted. "If nobody can go to the sun, how do they know how hot it is?"

I sighed. As Daddy always says, not everybody knows as much about science and outer space as we do!

"One way is to use a solar probe," I said. "That's a spacecraft made to get close to the sun or other stars so scientists can learn more about them. As a matter of fact, I've been working on one this summer. Here, I'll show you."

My half-built probe was on the counter, and covered to keep the dust off. I whipped off the sheet. The probe was made out of a big metal wastebasket. Sensors, antennae, and other instruments covered its surface.

Wallace looked impressed. "That's cool," he said. "Maybe Zixtar could drive it to the sun."

"No way," I said. "Even NASA hasn't tried making solar probes that people can travel in. The technology isn't there yet."

"That's okay," Wallace said. "Remember, *Comet Jumpers* is set in the year 3000. Use your imagination! I'm sure scientists will work it out by then." He grabbed something off the counter. "What's this?"

"Be careful!" I grabbed it back. "They're the goggles Daddy and I made for viewing solar eclipses."

I put the goggles in my space pack for safekeeping and opened my favorite book, *The Universe*, to the chapter about solar probes. I was explaining how carbon heat shields help protect from the sun's extreme heat and energy waves when I noticed that instead of paying attention, Wallace was scratching Astro Cat with Zixtar's tentacle.

"Are you listening?" I asked. "Our episode won't work if we don't get the facts right. I wish you'd think like a scientist more often!"

"I wish you'd build a time machine so we could see what the year 3000 is really like," Wallace said at the same time.

WHOOOSH!

"It's happening again!" I cried as Astro Cat yowled, the Baby squealed, and the room went dark—and then suddenly very, very bright . . .

Chapter 3

PRIMROSE

"I can't see!" Wallace shouted. "It's so bright in here!"

My eyes were squeezed tightly shut. I felt around for my space pack and pulled out my solar goggles. Once they were on, I carefully opened my eyes.

We were in a spacecraft! All four of us were strapped into comfy chairs. Astro Cat and the Baby were sharing theirs. The Baby looked thrilled as he tickled Astro

Cat's whiskers. Astro Cat looked much less thrilled. Between Wallace and me was a large cube, like a table, with doors on the sides and a smooth, shiny top.

There were huge windows encircling us. On one side were stars and distant planets.

On the other side was nothing but a fiery yellow glare.

"Where are we?" I asked.

The cube hummed, and the top glowed aqua blue. A voice emerged from it. It sounded a little like Mary Poppins.

"Now exiting jump-drive mode. Location: orbiting star of spectral class G2, luminosity class V, known as—"

"I know where we are!" I blurted out. "We're orbiting the sun in a solar probe!"

Wallace carefully squinted through one eye. "Hey, I think my eyes are adjusting," he said. "And wow, cool, a solar probe! But wait, you said there's no such thing as one people can ride in."

"There isn't," I said. "It's impossible with current technology."

Wallace looked intrigued. "Maybe we're

in the future. Hey, computer, what year is this?"

The cube spoke again. "It is the Earth year 3000."

"Wow!" Wallace cried. He unbuckled himself and leaped out of his chair. "That's the year of *Comet Jumpers*! Hey, Zixtar, now you're not just an interstellar pirate—you're a time traveler, too!"

I didn't know what to say. Sure, Einstein believed time travel was possible. But I never thought I'd see it happen. Then again, Wallace wasn't floating around. That meant the probe had artificial gravity, which didn't exist in our time. And he wasn't going blind from the glare, and neither was the Baby or Astro Cat. That meant the windows were probably made out of something that hadn't been invented yet. I carefully lifted my goggles. Were we really in the future?

Wallace kept talking. "And this computer is just like the one on the smuggler's ship in episode forty-seven," he said. "Its name was Blackbeard, and it could make the ship disappear!"

I barely heard him. I was staring out

the windows. Was that really the sun out there? It felt weird to be so close to it. I guessed the probe must have powerful carbon heat shields.

Wallace was still talking about *Comet Jumpers*. He pulled out his notebook and started jotting things down.

"Hey, computer," he said. "Do you have a name?"

"My name is PRIMROSE," the cube said. "That stands for Primary Research Interstellar Mobile Rocket Orbiting Star Enterprise. I am state-of-the-art and here to assist."

Just then the Baby started to wail. He wiggled and waved his arms, trying to get loose from his chair.

As I got up and freed him, PRIMROSE spoke again: "Please repeat—your words are indecipherable. Searching language database."

When I set the Baby on the floor, he squealed happily.

"Apologies," PRIMROSE said. "Your words have not been found in my database of twelve million known languages."

Wallace laughed. "Silly PRIMROSE! He's not speaking a language. He's a baby!"

Astro Cat jumped down, too. He meowed.

PRIMROSE spoke again: "Request received. Please stand by."

"Huh?" Wallace said. "What request?"

A moment later, one of the doors in the cube opened, revealing a plate of tuna. A robotic arm emerged and set the plate on the floor. Astro Cat purred and started to eat.

"Whoa!" Wallace exclaimed.
"PRIMROSE speaks Cat!"

"That's pretty cool," I said. "Also, I bet
there's some kind of super-advanced 3D
printer inside that thing, sort of like the
one Daddy and I are building. Ours can't
make food, though. Let's test what else it
can do!"

"I could use a new pencil," Wallace
suggested.

That seemed a little boring to me, but
I went along with it. "PRIMROSE, please
send us a pencil," I said.

"Request received," PRIMROSE replied. "Please stand by."

Soon the robotic arm was setting a pencil on the floor. Astro Cat sniffed it, then returned to his tuna.

"Sweet!" Wallace said, grabbing the pencil. "Hey, Val, let's add a computer like PRIMROSE to our script!"

New idea:

Computer with cool name that means lots of stuff. It can create anything—even a giant saltshaker to melt the ice aliens!

I glanced at what Wallace had written. "Hey, that's thinking like a scientist!" I said. "Salt melts ice, and having the ice aliens melt will look great in the TV show. Now our story is really getting good!"

"Thanks," Wallace said. "I'm glad *somebody* thinks I know how to tell a story."

"What do you mean?" I asked.

He didn't say anything for a moment. But when I poked him, he finally answered. "This past Easter, I told my first story at the family storytelling contest," he said. "It was a great one about the *Comet Jumpers* Beamatron malfunctioning and making everyone end up with the wrong heads on the wrong bodies. But I guess it didn't come out in words the same way I imagined it. Because nobody understood what I was talking about. Dwayne and my other cousins have been making fun of me ever since."

"Sounds like that story was just an experiment that went wrong," I told him. "It happens all the time in science. Even to me."

"Really?" Wallace said.

Before I could respond, red lights started flashing all over the probe. "ALERT! ALERT!" PRIMROSE blared. "Solar flare incoming! Strap in and prepare for immediate impact!"

Chapter 4

SOLAR FLARE

"You heard PRIMROSE!" I shouted. "Strap in, everyone. Quick!"

I grabbed the Baby, and Wallace grabbed Astro Cat. Once they were strapped in, we buckled our own seat belts—just in time!

First, the whole ship lurched. It felt like the time I got caught in a huge wave at the beach.

Then airbags popped out of our chairs

and enveloped us. I was glad since the ship started tumbling end over end like a wild amusement park ride. The Baby cheered.

"What's happening?" Wallace cried.

"PRIMROSE just told us—it's a solar flare!" I replied. "That's a burst of high energy X-rays and gamma rays. It's like a million nuclear bombs going off!"

The flare seemed to last forever, but finally the ship stopped tumbling. The airbags deflated.

"Hey, PRIMROSE," I said. "Is it safe to unbuckle now?"

The computer didn't answer for a moment.

"PRIMROSE?" Wallace said. "Are you there?"

A weird laugh emerged from the speakers. Wallace and I looked at each other. Before we could say anything, the computer finally spoke.

"Please stand by," it said. But it didn't sound like PRIMROSE anymore. The voice sounded less like Mary Poppins and more like a cowboy from the old Western movies Daddy watches sometimes.

Wallace laughed. "Okay, we'll stand by, pardner!"

The computer spoke again: "I have good news and bad news." It still sounded like a cowboy talking, but once in a while a word would come out in PRIMROSE's voice. "The bad news is, some of my newfangled circuits were damaged by the flare."

Uh-oh! That did sound like bad news. I noticed that Wallace looked confused.

"The energy from a solar flare can damage electronics and satellites," I told him. "It even happens on Earth sometimes when there's a big flare."

"Okay," Wallace said. "So what's the good news?"

The computer responded: "The good news is that all entertainment and food production systems are A-OK! Hang on to your Stetsons and I'll show ya."

Loud opera music poured out of the speakers. The Baby squealed with delight and waved his arms in time to the music. Then the floor changed to look like a playground, with hopscotch and four square boxes chalked in.

The 3D printer started humming. "Maybe it's making a ball so we can play four square," Wallace said eagerly.

"We don't have time for four square!" I exclaimed. "We have to figure out how to fix this. Think like a scientist!"

The door on one side of the cube popped open. A whole eggplant was sitting there.

"That's not a ball," Wallace said. "It's an eggplant. And it's not even cooked! So much for the super-duper high-tech 3D printer, huh?"

I ignored him. The probe's computer was damaged, and that could be a disaster. I had no idea how far the solar flares had sent us into deep space. Astronaut Girl always knows what to do, but this time I was worried.

Before I could figure out a plan, the computer spoke again: "Howdy, pardners. Cinch yourselves back in your seats because jump drive will commence in ten seconds. Ten . . . nine . . ."

"Jump drive?" Wallace and I said at the same time.

I'd heard of jump drive, of course. Scientists imagined it could be a way to travel faster than the speed of light. Were we really about to do that? If so, where were we going?

"Hold on a second!" I blurted out, as I strapped the Baby back into his chair.

But the computer was still counting: ". . . six . . . five . . . four . . ."

Chapter 5

JUMP DRIVE

"...three...two...one!"

BOOM! Suddenly a huge force pressed me against the back of my seat. The probe shook, and the windows showed only darkness.

"What's happening?" Wallace shouted.

"Maybe since it's damaged, the probe is taking us home," I guessed.

A second later, we stopped shaking. Three stars appeared outside the windows.

One was very bright.

"I don't think it took us home," Wallace said. "What's a jump drive, anyway? Is it like the Beamatron on *Comet Jumpers*?"

"I told you, the Beamatron is fake," I said. "But some scientists are trying to invent stuff like jump drives. That would make it possible to travel faster than the speed of light."

"I know what that is," Wallace said. "They talk about it on *Comet Jumpers* all the time. It's the speed that light travels through space."

"That's right," I said, a little impressed. "The speed of light is more than six hundred million miles per hour. At the speed of light, someone could travel around the earth seven and a half times in one second."

"Cool, like a superhero!" Wallace pulled out his notebook and scribbled a few words.

I looked at the stars outside. "I wonder where we landed," I said.

A burst of static came from the computer. Then a new voice spoke: *"Bonjour, mes enfants!"* it exclaimed.

Wallace laughed. "Hey, I think PRIMROSE is speaking French now!"

The computer started gabbing away in French. I didn't understand most of it. But suddenly I heard a familiar word.

"Wait, did she just say *Polaris*?" I blurted out.

Wallace shrugged. "It sounded like *polar bear* to me."

"No, I think she's talking about Polaris—that's the North Star." I pointed out a window. "I bet that's where we are! See?

Actually there are three stars, and Polaris is the brightest."

The Baby started fussing. Wallace got up and unbuckled him and Astro Cat. I stood up, too.

"Wow, I can't believe we're this close to the North Star!" I exclaimed.

"Gramps showed me how to find the North Star when I was four years old," Wallace said. "That's when he taught me all the constellations. The North Star is part of Ursa Minor, which means 'little bear.' Once Carlos and I got lost in the woods when we were camping, and we used the North Star to find our way back."

"I'm not sure that's going to work this time," I said. "We're a lot farther from home than we were before the jump drive."

The Baby wasn't paying attention to Polaris. He crawled over, patted the side of the computer, and cooed.

"I think the Baby's bored," Wallace said. "Maybe PRIMROSE can make a toy."

The computer responded in French. Then the door opened. The eggplant was gone. Instead, soap bubbles started floating out. The probe's interior lighting flashed like a disco ball. That made the bubbles turn rainbow colored.

The Baby shrieked with delight. He tried to grab a large purple bubble. He missed, but Astro Cat leaped up and popped it with his claws.

Wallace laughed and grabbed Zixtar. "Attack of the intergalactic bubble monsters!" he exclaimed. "Save us, Zixtar!"

He made Zixtar pop a bubble with his tentacle. The Baby squealed and clapped his hands.

I couldn't believe they were all goofing off at a time like this. Didn't they realize we were in big trouble? The computer wasn't working right. We were trapped light-years from home in the year 3000. What were we going to do?

But I'm Astronaut Girl, and Astronaut Girl never gives up.

I looked at the computer screen that was the top of the cube. Maybe I could reprogram it and take over the jump-drive system to get us home.

The others were still playing with the soap bubbles. I ignored them and started working on the computer. Even though there were glitches from the solar-flare damage, it was still much faster and more powerful than any computer I'd used before. I quickly found a blueprint of the entire probe. That's when I discovered a big problem.

"Oh no!" I cried. "It's even worse than we thought. The computer shows that two of the heat shields are loose! It must have happened during the solar flare."

Wallace balanced a bubble on his nose. "What does that mean?"

"The shields protect us from the extreme heat of stars like that." I pointed out the window again at Polaris. "If we don't get  them fixed soon, the whole probe could turn into a giant baked potato!"

Chapter 6

PROBLEM SOLVING

I had to find a way to fix those heat shields!

"I wonder if this probe has robotic arms like the space station," I said, waving a soap bubble out of my face. "I could probably figure out how to use them to tighten the shields."

Wallace looked interested. "The high-school kids in my old town built a robotic arm for the science fair last year," he said.

"It was really cool. Carlos and I talked about adding one to Zixtar's spaceship."

"Great idea!" I said. "Robotic arms are super useful for fixing stuff in outer space."

I studied the blueprints on the computer. It didn't take long to locate the robotic arms. Next I had to figure out how to control them.

I searched the computer's database and found the section about robotic arms. When I pressed Activate, controls popped out of the wall of the probe. Astro Cat jumped in surprise, and the Baby giggled before going back to grabbing soap bubbles. A screen dropped from the ceiling. It showed a view of the arms as they emerged from the outside shell.

Wallace peered at the screen. "Awesome! I bet Zixtar could use those to grab an

ice-alien missile right out of the air!"

"There's no air in space," I said. I wasn't really paying attention to Wallace, though. The robotic arm controls were pretty simple, but I had to focus. I could see the loose heat shields on the screen sticking up above the rest. Each was about the size of a laptop computer.

I got to work, using the robotic arms to push the first tile gently back into place. Out of the corner of my eye, I could see Wallace scribbling in his notebook. It was a little distracting, but I did my best to ignore it.

New story idea for script—
Zixtar uses robotic
arms to grab ice-alien
commander and hurl
him into the sun. (That
way his tentacles won't
freeze!)

I heard Wallace giggling behind me. But I didn't look over. I just needed to tighten one more screw . . .

"Got it!" I yelled in triumph. "One down, one to go!"

I moved the robotic arms over to the second heat shield. Three corners were loose. The first corner was easy to fix, but the second one was a little trickier. I was still adjusting the controls to tackle it when PRIMROSE suddenly started speaking in French again.

"What's she saying now?" Wallace asked.

I shrugged, still focused on the heat shield. I moved the arms toward the second screw . . .

"Hey!" Wallace sounded worried. "Is she counting in French? What if we're going into jump drive again? Get back in your seat, hurry!"

He was already strapping in Astro Cat and the Baby. I wanted to finish my job, but I could hear the countdown, too. I barely made it to my seat before the ship began to shake and the windows went dark.

When the ship stopped shaking, a whole new star appeared outside the windows. "PRIMROSE, where did you take us now?" Wallace exclaimed.

"Don't bother, we won't understand her anyway," I said.

But when PRIMROSE responded, she wasn't speaking French anymore. Now she sounded like the weather guy on the news.

"Forecast says, dark and starry throughout deep space, especially in the area of the star Bellatrix," the computer said.

"Does that mean that's Bellatrix out there?" Wallace asked. "It looks kind of blue."

"It's a really interesting star," I told him. "It's much hotter and larger than our sun. Plus it's named after a woman—the name means 'female warrior' in Latin."

Wallace laughed. "A warrior star?" he said. "Maybe we should put that in our script! The sun could join Zixtar's army ..."

He kept talking, but I wasn't really listening. I wanted to get those last two screws tightened before PRIMROSE decided to take us even farther away.

I returned to the controls. But when I tried to move the robotic arms, they didn't respond. I tried again. Nothing happened.

"Oh no!" I cried. "I think the robotic arms got damaged by that last jump! Now how are we going to fix the last heat shield?"

Chapter 7

WALLACE'S NEW IDEA

Wallace was writing in his notebook again. I wasn't sure he'd even heard me.

"Wallace!" I cried. "Pay attention! This is really bad. If we don't fix this, we can't go home."

He finally looked up. "Why not? You're a good coder, right? So just write a code to override PRIMROSE and jump us back to Earth."

"I can try that, I guess," I said. "But I

can't write a code to tighten that heat shield. They *all* need to be working, or the probe won't survive reentry into Earth's atmosphere!"

"Oh." Now Wallace looked worried. "How do we fix it?"

"If the robotic arms were still working, it would be easy," I said. "So we need to fix

the arms first, but that could take a while—
and who knows how many more jumps the
shields can survive . . ."

"Okay, so why bother with robotic
arms?" Wallace held up his hands. "*We*
have arms—let's just use those! No coding
necessary!"

"You mean a spacewalk?" I said.

"Maybe," Wallace said. "What's that?"

"Any time an astronaut goes outside the ship while in space, that's a spacewalk," I told him. "That could be really risky, especially since we could go into jump drive at any moment."

"True," Wallace said. "But at least PRIMROSE always does a countdown. That gives us ten seconds of warning."

I thought about that. If Wallace stayed by the computer, he could radio to me as soon as the next countdown started.

"I'm not sure ten seconds is enough time," I said. "I would have to get back into the air lock, and—"

Wallace frowned. "Hang on," he interrupted. "Who says *you* get to do the spacewalk?"

I was surprised. Of course I should be the one to do it! I'm Astronaut Girl!

Before I could say that, the computer spoke again in its weather-guy voice: "Here's what to expect for the ten seconds ahead," it said. "Continued outside temperatures ranging between five million and negative 455 degrees Fahrenheit. Plus one hundred percent chance of jump drive in ten . . . nine . . . eight . . ."

Chapter 8

A BIG DECISION

"At ease, Privates," the computer barked when we came out of jump drive. "We've arrived in orbit around a blue-tinged white star known as Vega. Carry on!"

"Hey, now PRIMROSE sounds like an army commander," Wallace said. He made Zixtar salute with one tentacle. "Roger that, General PRIMROSE!"

"Vega!" I exclaimed. "That's one of the most studied stars. It was the first one other than the sun to be photographed and measured. Cool!"

Astro Cat started wiggling in his seat. The Baby gurgled.

"Maybe we should let them move around," Wallace said. He got up and released the two of them.

I stood up, too. As I did, my stomach let out a grumble.

"I'm hungry," I said. "Let's get those shields fixed so we can get home for the barbecue."

"What's the rush?" Wallace said. "Anyway, we still have to decide who gets to do the spacewalk."

I had a feeling Wallace was trying to avoid his family storytelling contest, so I decided not to argue with him. Besides, nobody could do a spacewalk until I figured out how to make it work.

The Baby crawled over to us and tried to grab Zixtar.

"Zixtar's not a toy," Wallace told the Baby. "Hey, General PRIMROSE, can't you entertain the crew somehow?"

"Roger that, Private," the computer responded.

The cube's door opened. A bright red laser pointer dot appeared on the floor.

Astro Cat leaped on the dot. The Baby giggled and chased him. Wallace laughed as the two of them pursued the red dot all over the floor.

I was glad they were distracted. That gave me a chance to work on the computer.

Wallace looked over at me. "What are you doing?" he asked.

"I'm trying to turn off the jump drive," I said. "But the navigation system seems totally fried. Even my coding skills might not be able to fix it."

"You don't have to fix the whole navigation system," Wallace said. "We just need more time on the next countdown so I can get back inside from my spacewalk."

I scowled. "*Your* spacewalk?" I said. "I don't think so. But hold on—give me a second to look for the countdown programming . . ."

It took only a few minutes to find it. There wasn't a way to make the countdown longer. But I had another idea.

"Maybe I can program the computer to restart as soon as the next countdown begins," I said. "That should delay things for at least another thirty seconds."

Wallace looked worried. "That's not much extra time."

He was right, it wasn't. Could I get back in through the air lock in less than a minute?

Then I realized something. My heart sank.

"I can't do the spacewalk," I blurted out. "I need to be here to do the programming. You'll have to do it."

Wallace gulped. *"Me?"*

I couldn't believe this was happening. I'd been dreaming about doing a spacewalk my whole life.

But I tried not to think about that. "You'll need to wear a space suit and helmet to let you breathe," I told Wallace. "You can talk to me through the radio, and I'll tell you exactly what you need to do."

He took a deep breath. "Can Zixtar come along as my second-in-command?"

"Sure, I guess so," I said. "Just make sure you attach him to your suit so he doesn't float away. By the way, you'll also be tethered to the probe with ropes so you can't drift off into space."

"That's good," Wallace said with a shaky laugh.

I could tell he was scared. "Don't worry, Wallace," I said. "If Commander Neutron can do a spacewalk to rescue some silly fake alien on *Comet Jumpers*, you can do it, too."

"Well, Gramps always tells me that Babe Ruth said not to let the fear of striking out hold you back," Wallace said.

"Who's Babe Ruth?" I asked.

Wallace looked shocked. "You don't know Babe Ruth? He's only the most famous baseball player of all time!"

69

"Whatever. Let's get you suited up," I said.

I helped him get into his space suit. He carefully clipped Zixtar to his belt.

"This holds your jet thrusters," I said, handing him a space pack. "It'll help you move around out there. You control it with this." I tossed him a small joystick.

He nodded and stepped to the air-lock door. "Promise me one thing, Val," he said. "If I don't make it back, you'll finish our *Comet Jumpers* script and enter it in the contest."

"Don't be silly," I said. "You'll make it back so we can finish it together."

"No, really." He sounded serious. "Promise."

I crossed my heart. "I promise," I said. "I'll be in constant contact on the radio. Good luck out there."

I opened the air lock. He strapped on his helmet, held on to Zixtar, and stepped through the door.

Chapter 9

THE SPACEWALK

The air-lock door clunked shut behind Wallace. "Can you hear me?" I said into the computer.

"I hear you." Wallace's voice sounded funny through the radio. "What happens now?"

I could see him on the screen. His face peeking through the helmet looked nervous.

"Clip your tether to the hook by the door," I told him. "In a few seconds, the outside air-lock door will open. Once you're outside, clip the second tether to the hook out there."

"Got it," Wallace said.

I watched on the screen as Wallace followed my instructions. Soon he was tethered to the outside of the probe.

"Way to go," I said. "You're doing a spacewalk!"

I was excited for him, but I still wished it was me out there. One day I would get my chance.

"It's hard to move around," Wallace said. "Now I know how the Baby feels. My legs are useless. Even the jet thrusters only help a little. I have to pull myself around with my hands to get anywhere!"

"Crawl toward the loose heat shield," I said. "It's the one sticking up just ahead."

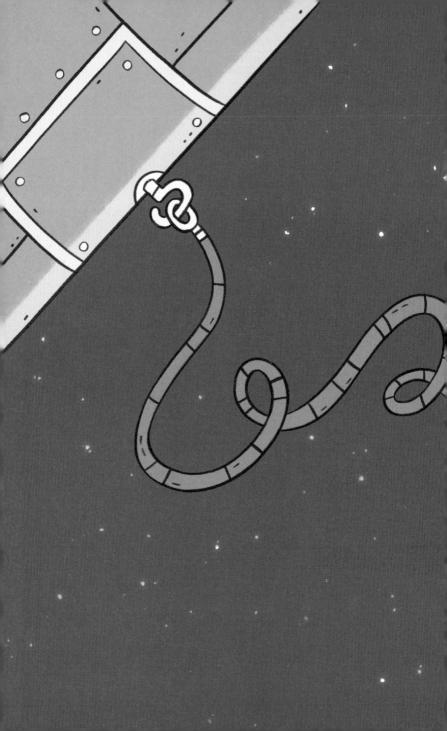

"I see it," he said. "It's not too far."

Just then the Baby started crying loudly.

"What's going on in there?" Wallace asked.

"It's just the Baby," I said. "He always gets cranky when he's hungry. I think he's saying hurry up and fix the heat shield so we can get to that barbecue."

"Okay, okay," Wallace said. "I think I found the right tool . . ."

I strapped the Baby and Astro Cat into their seat to keep them quiet. Then I watched on the screen as Wallace tightened one of the bolts.

"Nice job," I said. "One more to go."

"Okay." Wallace shifted toward the last loose bolt. But he missed the handhold. "Yikes!" he cried, sounding scared.

He grabbed the handhold with his other

hand. That meant letting go of his tool.

"Quick, grab it before it floats away!" I cried.

But it was too late. We both watched the tool float off into space.

"Oops," Wallace said. "Now what do I do?"

"Maybe there's a backup in your pack," I said.

He dug into the pack with his free hand. Then he shook his head. "I don't see anything in here that will work."

"Well, figure something out!" I exclaimed. "Think like a scientist!"

"I'm *not* a scientist!" he cried. "I don't know what to do! Maybe I should just come back in."

I couldn't believe he was giving up. I really wished it was me out there.

"Come on, Zixtar, let's get back inside before there's another jump drive," Wallace said. Then he gasped. "Wait, I just had a great idea!"

"What great idea?" I asked.

"Attention, Privates!" the computer barked out. "Prepare for jump drive in ten . . . nine . . ."

"Wallace, the countdown is starting!"

My fingers flew over the computer screen. "Okay, the computer is restarting, but it won't take long. You need to get back in here. Pronto!"

"I think one of Zixtar's tentacles is the right size to tighten the bolt," Wallace said. "This should only take a second . . ."

"Wallace?" I said. "Get back inside!"

He didn't answer. On the screen, I saw him huddled over the heat shield. I glanced at the computer. The restart was almost finished.

"Wallace!" I cried. "If you don't head for the air lock soon, you won't make it. We'll have to fix it after the next jump."

"Almost done," he said.

". . . eight," the computer said, ". . . seven . . . six . . ."

Outside, Wallace was finally scooting toward the air lock. I strapped myself into my seat and held my breath as he pulled himself inside.

". . . three . . . two . . ."

CLUNK! The outer air-lock door shut behind him.

"We made it!" he cried, just as the ship went into jump drive.

Chapter 10

STAR STORIES

As soon as the jump finished, I rushed over to let Wallace out of the air lock.

"Are you okay?" I cried.

Wallace grinned from ear to ear. "I'm fine," he said, rubbing his shoulder. "But next time I'd rather be strapped safely into my chair."

I grinned back. "I'm just glad you made it inside."

"Zixtar, too!" Wallace held up the action

figure. "He was a real hero out there."

"You both were," I told him.

I let Astro Cat and the Baby loose, then looked out a window. There were two stars outside. One was a big, bright white star, and the other was much smaller and dimmer. They looked kind of familiar . . .

"I guess we're still not home yet," Wallace said. "Hey, PRIMROSE, what star is that?"

WOOF! WOOF!

Loud barking poured out of the speakers. Astro Cat leaped straight up in the air. His tail puffed out, and his eyes went wide.

"It's okay, Astro Cat," I said. "That's not a real dog."

"Wow! And I thought PRIMROSE was hard to understand when she

was speaking French!" Wallace exclaimed with a laugh. "Too bad she can't help ID the star this time."

I thought about that. "Or can she?" I said. I pulled out *The Universe* and flipped through until I found the page I wanted. "I was just thinking that those two stars look like Sirius A and B," I told Wallace. "Also known as the Dog Star."

"Oh, I've heard of the Dog Star," he said. "That's part of Canis Major. It's the brightest star in the night sky."

"That's because it's one of the nearest stars to Earth," I said. "Which means at least we're getting closer to home—and your barbecue."

WOOF! The cube door slid open. Sitting there was a jar of PRIMROSE's Fabulous Finger-Lickin' BBQ Sauce.

Wallace picked it up. "Hey, this smells great," he said. "Actually, I'm getting pretty hungry. Maybe we should go back. But how?"

I cracked my knuckles. "Time to get coding and see if I can override the jump drive."

PRIMROSE didn't seem happy when I started messing with her programming. She kept barking and making all the lights blink on and off.

"Easy, PRIMROSE," Wallace said. "Be a good dog. We're just trying to get home."

I stayed focused and soon figured out the override command. "Setting coordinates for the sun."

PRIMROSE started barking again. This time the barking sounded rhythmical.

"I think that's the countdown," Wallace said. "Let's strap in."

He grabbed the Baby. I pulled Astro Cat out from under a chair. Soon we were all strapped in . . .

When we landed, I saw a large star outside a window. It looked familiar, but I wasn't sure . . .

"PRIMROSE, bark once if that's the sun, and twice if it's not," I said.

"Affirmative, we are orbiting the sun," PRIMROSE said in her original Mary Poppins voice. "Shall I repeat that in Canine?"

Wallace laughed with relief. "Hey, welcome back, PRIMROSE!" he said. "And since you asked, can you bark 'Take Me

Out to the Ball Game'?"

I smiled as PRIMROSE started barking. It was nice to see the sun again. After all, it's what makes life on Earth possible. It provides light and heat and photosynthesis, and it controls climate and weather.

But it was awfully bright this close up—so bright that I closed my eyes for a moment. When I opened them, we were back in my basement lab.

☆ ☆ ☆

The barbecue was lots of fun. Wallace's family was nice, and everyone loved the potato salad. We ate and talked and swam in the backyard pool since the rain had totally stopped by then.

When the sun went down, Wallace's

great-grandma Ruby said it was time for
the storytelling contest. Everybody took
turns. Some stories were funny, some were
exciting, and some were a little sad. Even
my mom told a story about the time she
found a rare orchid in an abandoned lot.

Wallace and I sat together listening to
all of them. "Are you going to take a turn
tonight?" I whispered to him as Kayla told
a story about meeting a mermaid. "You
have a great story to tell this time." I pulled
the solar goggles out of my pocket. "Just

tell them about our trip to the stars!"

"I don't know . . ." Wallace glanced toward Dwayne with a frown.

"Remember what Gabe Booth said," I told him. "Don't let fear of striking out hold you back."

He laughed. "You mean Babe Ruth?" he said. "Maybe you're right . . ."

I nodded. "You can't give up. I'm a great scientist, and you're a great storyteller."

When Kayla finished her story, I poked Wallace again. He grabbed the goggles, stood up, and raised his hand.

"I'll go next," he announced.

Dwayne snorted and elbowed the cousin sitting next to him. They both laughed.

I glared at them. "Go ahead, Wallace," I said.

And he did. He told the whole story of our adventure. He imitated all of PRIMROSE's voices, which made everyone laugh. Cousin Kayla even snorted soda out of her nose when he started barking!

When Wallace finished, everyone cheered. Dwayne jumped up and gave him a high five. Then Dwayne pulled off the medal he was wearing and put it around Wallace's neck.

"I think we have a winner," Dwayne said. "Any objections?"

Everyone cheered even louder. Gramps gave a thumbs-up.

"Thanks, guys," Wallace said. "But I couldn't have done it without my good friend Astronaut Girl."